MORE THAN 1.5 MILLION COPIES SOLD!

* ALA Notable Children's Book 2007

* *Booklist*, Editor's Choice, Best Books of 2006

* *Kirkus Reviews*, Best Books of 2006, Early Chapter Books

* *Book Links*, Best New Books for the Classroom, 2006

* New York Public Library's 100 Titles for Reading and Sharing 2006

* *People* magazine's Summer Reading

ivy + BEAN
NO NEWS IS GOOD NEWS

BOOK 8

written by annie barrows + illustrated by sophie blackall

chronicle books · san francisco

For Margo, who likes cheese and wax. —A. B.

For Bea and Bea, both exceedingly creative with wax
and everything else. —S. B.

Library of Congress Cataloging-in-Publication Data
Barrows, Annie.
Ivy and Bean : no news is good news / by Annie Barrows ; [illustrated by] Sophie Blackall.
p. cm. — (Ivy and Bean ; bk. 8)
Audience: Ages 6-10.
Summary: Ivy and Bean try to make money by writing a newspaper about Pancake
Court but the neighbors are not pleased to read about themselves.
ISBN: 978-0-8118-6693-4 (alk. paper)
1. Ivy (Fictitious character : Barrows)—Juvenile fiction. 2. Bean (Fictitious character :
Barrows)—Juvenile fiction. 3. Best friends—Juvenile fiction. 4. Neighbors—Juvenile
fiction. 5. Newspapers—Juvenile fiction. 6. Money-making projects for children—Ju-
venile fiction. [1. Best friends—Fiction. 2. Friendship—Fiction. 3. Moneymaking projects—Fiction. 4. Newspapers—Fiction. 5. Neighbors—Fiction.] I. Blackall, Sophie, ill. II.
Title. III. Series: Barrows, Annie. Ivy + Bean ; bk. 8.
PZ7.B27576Iwbg 2011
813.6—dc22
[Fic]
2010050836

Book design by Sara Gillingham.
Typeset in Blockhead and Candida.
The illustrations in this book were rendered in Chinese ink.

Manufactured in the United States of America.

10 9 8 7 6 5 4 3

This product conforms to CPSIA 2008.

Chronicle Books LLC
680 Second Street, San Francisco, California 94107

www.chroniclekids.com

CONTENTS

SQUISH, SQUISH, SQUISH 7

A CHEESY SUGGESTION 16

OUT OF BUSINESS 24

BREAKING THE NEWS 32

WHAT A DEAL! 45

BAD NEWS 56

RATS! SALAMI! WOW! 66

GUESS THE NAKED BABY 74

A HOT STORY 83

FACING THE MUSIC 94

THE PANCAKE FLIPS 104

THE WHOLE BALL OF WAX 116

SQUISH, SQUISH, SQUISH

Bean looked around the lunch table. Vanessa had it. She got it every day. Zuzu had it. Emma had it. Marga-Lee had it. Dusit and Eric had it. Even MacAdam had it. Everyone had it except Bean and Ivy.

While Bean watched, Vanessa opened her lunchbox and took out a small red ball. It was a ball of cheese, but nobody cared about the cheese. The cheese was totally unimportant. The important thing was the coating around the cheese. It was wax.

The wax was red. It was smooth. If you pulled on the secret string inside it, the wax split into two halves. You unfolded them and took the cheese out. Sometimes you took a bite of cheese. Mostly, you didn't. You rolled the wax between your hands until it was warm. Once it was warm, you could squish it. You could squish it and squish it. You could make it into a shape. You could put it on your face. You could hold it for the rest of the day, and it would get dirtier and dirtier, until finally it was a small brown lump. Then you could stick it in the middle of your table and say it was a booger.

"Lookit," said Vanessa, rolling her wax. "I'm making a soccer ball."

Maybe Mom surprised me, Bean thought. Maybe she sneaked a cheese ball in my lunch for a special surprise. She peeked in her lunchbox. Nope.

"Lookit," said Zuzu. She had made a little wax horn. "I'm a unicorn." She stuck it in the middle of her forehead.

Bean could grab the horn. She could grab it and run away with it and move to another country where she wouldn't get in trouble. She sighed.

Ivy poked her with an elbow. "Pretend you don't care," she whispered.

"Check this out," said Dusit. He stuck his wax underneath his nose so it looked like blood was dripping out. "Ms. Aruba-Tate's going to freak."

Bean turned to Eric, who was squishing his

wax flat. "Trade you my granola bar for your wax," she said. She waved the bar at him. "Mmm! Granola!"

He glanced at it. "Yuck. Lookit." He stuck the wax over his eye. "Do I look like a one-eye?"

"Why don't you put it in your ear?" said Bean. "Your mom will think your brains are dropping out." That's what Bean would do.

"No," said Eric. "I'm a one-eye."

"They're called Cyclops," said Ivy.

Bean turned to MacAdam. "How about a nice granola bar, MacAdam old buddy? I'll trade for your wax."

MacAdam shook his head. He held his red ball of cheese in front of his face and looked

at it. Then he bit it. Bean watched him chew wax and cheese. When he swallowed, she had to look away. What a waste of wax.

"Lookit," said Marga-Lee. She had made a mustache out of her wax.

Bean took a sad bite of granola bar. It was going to be a long lunch.

+ + + + + +

After school, Ivy and Bean slumped home. "What a day," said Ivy.

"Another day, another dollar," said Bean.

"What does that mean?" asked Ivy.

"I don't know," Bean admitted. "My mom says it sometimes."

"We don't have a dollar," Ivy pointed out.

"I know. Wish we did."

"If we had a dollar, we could buy our own cheese balls."

Bean shook her head. "No, we couldn't. They cost more than a dollar."

Ivy nodded. "Here's what I don't understand. Everyone else's parents get them cheese. Why don't ours?"

"We've got to keep trying," said Bean. "Aren't grown-ups always telling us we have to keep trying?"

Together, they trudged around the circle of Pancake Court until they got to Bean's house.

"Hi, sweetie," said Bean's mom. "Hi, Ivy. How was school?"

"Fine," said Bean. The real answer was too complicated. "What's for snack?"

"Fruit!" said Bean's mom. She always said that.

"Fruit," repeated Bean. "We don't want fruit. We want cheese."

"I don't want to hear about that cheese again," said Bean's mom. "Have some fruit."

"Fruit tastes better with cheese," said Ivy.

"Especially lowfat Belldeloon cheese in a special just-for-you serving size," said Bean. Lowfat Belldeloon cheese was the stuff inside the red wax.

"Lowfat Belldeloon cheese in a special just-for-you serving size costs five dollars for six little bitty pieces of cheese, so if you want it, you can pay for it yourself," said Bean's mom. She had said this several times before.

"Cheese is good for you," said Bean. She had said this before, too.

"Cheese is not good for you when it costs five dollars for six little bitty pieces," said Bean's mom.

"We'd eat more fruit if we had cheese to eat with it," said Bean.

"I love fruit and cheese together," said Ivy.

"There's plenty of cheese in the fridge," said Bean's mom.

"Not lowfat Belldeloon cheese in a special just-for-you serving size," Bean reminded her.

"I DON'T WANT TO HEAR ONE MORE WORD ABOUT THAT CHEESE!" yelled Bean's mom, stomping out of the kitchen.

"She's so touchy sometimes," said Bean.

Ivy lowered her voice. "She'd probably be in a better mood if she ate—" Ivy glanced at Bean and wiggled her eyebrows.

"Lowfat Belldeloon cheese in a special just-for-you serving size," they whispered together.

A CHEESY SUGGESTION

Really, Ivy and Bean didn't want to hear one
more word about cheese either. Words didn't
seem to be getting them anywhere. Ivy had
tried whispering "Lowfat Belldeloon cheese
in a special just-for-you serving size" in her
mother's ear in the middle of the night.
Her mother was supposed to wake up
in the morning wanting to buy cheese
for Ivy. Instead, her mother woke up
while Ivy was whispering and told her
to get back to bed pronto.

Bean put a sticky note in her mom's book. In her best and tiniest handwriting, she wrote, "Belldeloon cheese is good!" and stuck it over some other words. She figured if her mom read about Belldeloon cheese in a book, she'd buy some for Bean. Instead, Bean's mom told Bean to leave her books alone.

It was tiring, trying to make parents do what they should.

After they had eaten their fruit (boring) and some peanut butter (not as boring, but still) and a little bit of brown sugar (yum!), Bean and Ivy played Eraser Valley. Bean had 56 erasers in different shapes. Most of them were animals, like bears and pigs, but she also had foods, like french fries and toast. Sometimes Ivy and Bean set up shops and restaurants and schools in Eraser Valley, and life was good for all the happy erasers. But mostly, Eraser Valley was disaster central. There were tsunamis and there were tornadoes. There were avalanches, earthquakes, and plagues. Eraser Valley had been through it all.

Bean and Ivy lined the erasers up and looked at them. What would befall Eraser Valley today?

"We could sell them," said Ivy.

"Hey! They're my erasers," Bean said. She picked up a sushi and held it tight. "I like them. Not for sale."

"I thought you wanted wax," Ivy said.

"I *do* want wax."

"Then we need money," Ivy argued. "We have to sell something."

"Nancy makes money babysitting," Bean said. Nancy was Bean's older sister. She was rich. "Do you think anyone would leave a baby with us?"

Ivy made a face. "What if it cried?"

Bean made a worse face. "What if it pooped?"

"Yuck. Forget it. We've got to sell something." Ivy was determined. "What's it going to be?"

Bean thought of a solution. "Let's sell some of Nancy's stuff."

"Isn't that stealing?" asked Ivy.

"Nah. Not really. Only a little." Bean shrugged. "She won't mind."

"Really?"

Bean thought about the time she had borrowed one tiny spool of wire from Nancy's bead kit. Which Nancy wasn't even using and Bean had really needed. And which Bean would have given back, if Nancy hadn't found it in Bean's room first and completely freaked out. "Okay, maybe not."

"What can we sell?" Ivy asked. She picked up a toast eraser. "I bet we could get a quarter for this."

"You're almost a witch," Bean pointed out. "Can't you magically make money?"

Ivy thought about it. "I've never heard of witches making money with magic."

"Why not?" Bean asked. "Even witches need money."

"Wait!" Ivy slapped her head. "Duh! Witches make money by selling potions!"

"Well, heck!" said Bean. She stood up, causing a major earthquake in Eraser Valley. "What are we waiting for?"

OUT OF BUSINESS

Ivy had been practicing to become a witch for a long time. She was going to be one when she grew up, for sure. She had already learned a lot of important witch things, like spells and potions. Especially potions. Potions were fun

because you had to mix ingredients to make them. Ingredients for potions were things like bugs and hair and leaf juice and rust. Ivy's collection of ingredients stood on a shelf in a special section of her room she called the magic lab.

Ivy took her magic book from its hiding place and flipped through the pages, looking for a potion to sell. It had to be something that people would want to buy.

"What do people want?" she asked.

"Horses," said Bean. She wanted a horse.

Ivy looked in her book. "Here's one for making your horse as fast as an eagle."

Bean rolled her eyes. "That's not much help if you don't have a horse."

Ivy nodded. Then she giggled. "Here's one that makes the first person you touch fall in love with you."

"Eeeww, gross! Touching." Bean shivered.

"Maybe we could sell it to Nancy," suggested Ivy.

"Too mean," said Bean.

"To Nancy?" asked Ivy.

"No! To whoever touched her! Geez!"

"Okay." Ivy looked through more pages. Then she stopped.

"This is a good one. A flying potion. Hey, and flies are one of the ingredients! I've got tons of flies!" She looked at the bottle of dead flies on her shelf.

"That's perfect," Bean said. "Everyone wants to fly. I bet we could charge ten dollars a bottle for a flying potion."

"Ten dollars. That's two bags of Belldeloon cheese," said Ivy.

"That's twelve pieces of wax," said Bean.

+ + + + + +

"Yuck," said Leo the next day at lunch recess.

"But you'll *fly*," said Bean, flapping her arms up and down to show flying.

"What are those black things?" he asked, looking at the jar of potion. It had turned out sort of yellowish, except for the bits that were black.

"Secret," said Bean.

"Flies," said Ivy at the same moment.

"Gross!" he said. "Nobody's going to drink that. You guys are nuts!"

Ivy and Bean looked at each other and sighed. The potion business was not so good. No one wanted the potion, not even at the special sale price of one dollar. Eric said that he would give Bean a quarter if *she* drank it, but she decided not to. A quarter wasn't enough to buy Belldeloon cheese anyway.

Lunch was almost over. They needed a potion-buyer on the double. Vanessa walked by, a lump of red wax in one hand and her brother Toby in the other. Even though he was only in kindergarten, he had a lump of red wax, too.

It was worth a try. "Hey, Toby, trade you a flying potion for your wax!" called Bean. He turned around and looked at her. She waved the jar of potion. "Don't you want to fly?" She waved the jar some more. "Look, I can hardly keep it in my hand! It's trying to fly away!" She gave the jar a little toss. "See? It's—" The jar slipped through her fingers and crashed against the cement of the breezeway. Ivy and Bean stared at a million pieces of glass sitting in a puddle of dead flies and yellow glop.

"Just what do we have here, young ladies?"

Ivy and Bean turned
around. It was Rose the
Yard Duty. The potion
business went from bad
to worse.

BREAKING THE NEWS

That afternoon, Bean's dad wandered into the kitchen. "Holy moly cannoli, what are you eating?" he squawked.

"Gmckr tnch," said Bean. Her mouth was full. "Ff bplzrp npnd rr."

"Graham cracker sandwich," explained Ivy. "With maple syrup and peanut butter."

"Wow," said Bean's dad. He sat down at the table to watch.

Bean swallowed. It took a long time. Finally, she said, "Dad. Can we have some money?"

"You get an allowance."

Bean sighed. "No, I don't. Not for two more months. Don't you remember?"

His eyes got narrow. He remembered. "Serves you right."

Bean didn't want to talk about *that*. Quickly, she asked, "But what if I need some money?"

"Earn it!" he said. "When I was a kid, I didn't get extra money from my parents. If I wanted a comic book, I had to buy it myself. With money I earned myself."

"But how did you make the money? Did you have a job?"

"Sure. I had a bunch of jobs. I washed my father's car, for instance. And mowed the lawn. And vacuumed the house." He paused. "And there was the newspaper, too."

Ivy and Bean looked at each other. *Car*, mouthed Ivy silently.

"We'll wash your car for ten dollars," said Bean at once.

"No," said her father.

"What do you mean, no?" yelped Bean. "You just told us we should make money by washing cars."

"Hello? Do you remember the time you washed the house? Do you remember what happened in the basement?" he said. "No water."

Bean rolled her eyes. "Okay, okay. Lawn."

"Ha!" Her father snorted. "You think I'm going to let you drive a lawn mower? Think again."

"Vacuuming?" said Ivy.

"Excuse me?" he said. "Aren't you the ones who vacuumed up the tuna salad?"

Bean sighed deeply. "Fine. What was the newspaper?"

"I made a news-paper," said Dad. He smiled. "It was called *The Explosion.*"

"Cool! Did it explode?" Bean asked. That sounded like a pretty good newspaper.

"No, no. That's just what it was called," her dad said. He leaned back in his chair and stared into space. "It was about all the stuff that happened in my neighborhood. You know, who'd gotten a dog, who'd fallen off their bike, that kind of news." He started to look dreamy. "It was great. Everyone wanted it. I charged a quarter a copy. Which was a lot of money back then. I went to all the houses in my neighborhood.

I remember exactly what I said, too. I said, 'Hello, I'm David. Do you want to know what's going on in the world around you? Subscribe to *The Explosion* and you'll learn about all the thrilling events that happen on Aspen Avenue. Plus, you'll be helping to keep a neighborhood child off the streets.'"

"What's subscribe mean?" asked Ivy.

"That means they gave me the money." Bean's dad still looked dreamy. "And then I brought them the newspaper when it was done."

Bean sat up straight. "They gave you the money first?"

"Yup."

"How much money did you make?" asked Bean.

"Lots," he said. "I don't remember."

"More than ten dollars?"

"I guess," he said. "Everyone bought it."

"Dad," said Bean. "Let me get this straight: You went around your neighborhood asking for money, and people just gave it to you? You didn't have to give them *The Explosion* first?"

Her dad shook his head. "No. They gave me the money, and then I made the newspaper."

Ivy looked at Bean. It sounded too good to be true.

"Are you sure, Dad?"

"Sure I'm sure," he said. "That's what subscribing is."

Bean looked at Ivy and shrugged. Dads don't lie. Both girls stood up. "Thanks for making such a great snack, Dad! See ya!" said Bean.

"Wait. Don't you want to hear about what I wrote?" asked Bean's dad. But Ivy and Bean were already gone.

+ + + + + +

Bean sat down with a thump in her basket chair. "Bet we could charge a dollar."

"Your dad only charged a quarter," Ivy reminded her. She was stretched out on the floor.

"But that was back in the old days," said Bean. "And besides, our newspaper will be great. It'll be worth a dollar."

"What should we call it?" asked Ivy.

"*The Explosion*!" said Bean.

"No, that would be copycatting," Ivy said.

"Okay," Bean said. "How about *The Wax*?" After all, wax was the whole point of the newspaper.

Ivy frowned. "I don't think most people like wax as much as we do."

"Well, you think of something."

"I am thinking," Ivy said. She put her feet up on Bean's wall so that all her blood would go into her head and help her brain.

Suddenly Bean slid out of her basket chair and collapsed onto the rug. "*The Flipping Pancake*! Get it? Because it's Pancake Court! Isn't that great?" Sometimes her ideas were so good she amazed herself.

"*The Flipping Pancake*," said Ivy slowly. "*The Flipping Pancake*." She took her feet down off the wall. "It's perfect. Everyone who lives here will buy it."

"We'll be rich, rich, rich!" cackled Bean.

"We'll be rolling in wax!" cackled Ivy.

WHAT A DEAL!

The first stop was Kalia's house. Kalia was only two, so she couldn't read *The Flipping Pancake*, but Kalia had parents. Both Kalia's parents were named Jean, which Bean thought was hilarious. Jean the girl answered the door.

"Hi, Bean," she said. "What can I do for you?" A terrible scream came from upstairs.

"Is that Kalia?" asked Ivy.

"Is she okay?" asked Bean.

"She's fine," said Jean. "She's napping."

Bean cleared her throat. It was time for her speech. "Hello, I'm Bean," she said. Another terrible scream rang through the house. Bean talked louder. "Would you like to know the latest exciting news about Pancake Court? For only one dollar, you can get one thrilling issue of *The Flipping Pancake.* And you'll be helping to keep two neighborhood children off the streets." She smiled at Jean with all her teeth, just like the people on television.

"All for the bargain price of one dollar," said Ivy. That was her part.

Upstairs, something heavy crashed to the floor.

Together, Ivy and Bean began to sing, "Get the news of Pancake Court! Pancake Court! Pancake Court! All the news of Pancake Court! For! Only! A dollar!" Ads on television usually had songs.

"Sure." Jean was looking at the ceiling.
"Sure. A dollar. Hang on a sec!" She zipped
down the hall. Ivy and Bean waited on the
doorstep, listening to something hit a wall and
break into lots of pieces. Jean zipped back.

"Great! Here!" She handed Ivy a dollar just as the next scream blazed through the house. "Bye!" she said, shutting the door. They heard her running up the stairs.

"Wow. Aren't you glad we decided not to babysit?" said Bean.

Ivy nodded and stuck the dollar in her pocket. "One dollar down, nine to go."

The next house was Mrs. Trantz's. Mrs. Trantz's yard had sparkly white stones and big silver bubbles and teeny fences around every rosebush. It looked like someone nice

lived there, but that was a big lie. If Bean even so much as put one foot on Mrs. Trantz's pink front path, Mrs. Trantz whipped out the front door and started yelling.

"Forget it. Not worth it," said Ivy.

Bean nodded. Whew.

They moved on to Jake the Teenager's house. Jake the Teenager was in the garage beside his house. They knew he was in there because loud music with bad words in it was leaking out of the garage windows. Jake the Teenager didn't seem like the type to be interested in *The Flipping Pancake*, so Ivy and Bean didn't go to the garage. They went to the front door of the house. Bean was surprised that Jake the Teenager's dad heard the doorbell over the music, but he did. Bean hollered her speech as loud as she could, and Jake the Teenager's dad nodded and smiled. But just when Ivy was about to say "All for the bargain price of one dollar!" a really amazingly bad word came flying out of the garage, and she lost her mind. "Give us some money!" she screeched.

Jake the Teenager's dad nodded very fast and pulled three dollars out of his pocket. "Go, go!" he bellowed. "Run away!" He waved his hands, shooing them away before they could hear any more bad words. They didn't even get to do their song.

When they got down to the sidewalk, Bean looked at the three dollars. "Do we have to give him three copies of *The Flipping Pancake*?"

"No," said Ivy. She thought. "I think he gave us extra to forget that bad word."

"It's working!" said Bean. "I can't even remember it."

Ivy and Bean looked at each other and giggled.

After Jake the Teenager's house came Fester the dog's house. No one was home but Fester. He howled when they rang the doorbell, but he couldn't answer.

Next, Ruby and Trevor's mother gave them a dollar before Bean had even finished her speech. Of course Ivy's mother subscribed. She paid for two copies. Katy and Liana's father said he'd always wanted to know what was going on in Pancake Court.

At Dino and Crummy Matt's house, their mother said she wished that her children were so hard working. She said it really loud, so Dino and Crummy Matt could hear her over their video game. Ivy and Bean smiled modestly as she handed them a dollar.

It was easy, giving speeches, singing songs, taking money. It was easy *and* fun. "I don't know why my mom and dad complain about going to work," said Bean as they left Mr. Columbi's house. "It doesn't seem like such a big deal to me."

"Careful of the car!" yelled Mr. Columbi from his front porch. He was always worried about his car.

Bean waved and smiled and stuffed Mr. Columbi's dollar in her pocket.

"I bet we could make even more money," said Ivy, looking at Sophie W.'s house.

"Why? We have ten dollars. That's enough for two bags of Belldeloon cheese," Bean pointed out.

"I guess you're right," said Ivy. "We don't want to get worn out."

BAD NEWS

"I can't believe that's what you wanted to buy with your hard-earned money," said Bean's dad. "Cheese!"

Bean and Ivy didn't answer. They were happy. Each of them had a little red bag of Belldeloon cheese hooked over her wrist. The bags bounced against their legs as they walked across the parking lot. It felt nice.

"Why do you want cheese?" he asked.

"We like cheese," said Bean. There was no reason to tell him about the wax. He wouldn't understand.

"Especially lowfat Belldeloon cheese in a special just-for-you serving size," murmured Ivy, getting into the car.

They sat quietly in the backseat as Bean's dad drove them home. They had planned everything out. They were going to wait until they got home to open their bags. They would each eat just one cheese ball that afternoon. Then they would switch off cheese days. Ivy was going to go first. Tomorrow, she would bring a Belldeloon ball to school. The next day, Bean would bring a Belldeloon ball. The cheese-bringer would split her wax with the non-cheese-bringer. Ivy was going to use her half circle of wax to make a tiny voodoo doll. Bean wanted to squish hers in front of Vanessa. For ten days, they were going to drive everyone in Emerson School crazy. It was going to be great.

"So!" called Bean's dad from the front seat. "When are you going to start your writing?"

Ivy and Bean didn't answer. They were thinking about wax.

"Girls!"

"What?" said Bean dreamily.

"You're going to start writing when we get home, right?" he asked.

"What?"

"Stop saying what! Your magazine! You're going to start writing it today, right?"

"Magazine?"

"The magazine! The newspaper!" he yelled. "The one you sold! *The Flopping Pancake!*"

"Oh yeah. That," Bean said. "You don't have to yell."

"Well? Are you going to start today?" He was still yelling a little.

"After we have some cheese," said Bean. "Maybe."

Bean's dad pulled into the driveway. He stopped the car and then he turned around to look at Bean and Ivy with narrow eyes. "Before you have some cheese," he said. "For sure."

Dang.

+ + + + + +

"Okay. We did it. Can we have our cheese?" Bean said, coming into the kitchen with Ivy. "Where'd you hide the bags?"

Her dad looked up from his computer. "Let's see this newspaper first."

Bean handed him a piece of paper. At the top, it said *The Flipping Pancake* in enormous pink letters. Below that were some other words. Bean's dad read them out loud. "Everyone on Pancake Court will be happy to know that Ivy and Bean just got Lowfat Belldeloon cheese in a special just-for-you serving size. It costs five dollars a bag. But it's worth it! Weather today: Cloudy." He looked up at Bean.

"See, we did the weather, too. Can we have our cheese?" she asked.

"Bernice Blue, do you really think this is your best work?" he asked.

Oooh! Trick question! Grown-ups were sly.
If you said No, they got mad. If you said Yes,
they got mad. But you had to say something.

"Yes!" Bean said firmly.

"I don't think so," said her dad. He gave her a serious look.

Bean tried another way. She made her eyes big. "We did the best we could," she said in a little voice. Ivy made her eyes big, too, and nodded sadly.

Her father frowned at her. "I don't think so," he said again sternly. "Listen, girls, you promised people news about Pancake Court. You took their money. You have to deliver what you promised. Once you've made a real newspaper, with real news, you can have your cheese. Not before."

"That's not fair!" cried Bean.

"It's perfectly fair," he said, frowning some more.

"How are we supposed to find news about Pancake Court?" Bean squawked. "Nothing ever happens around here."

"Nonsense," her father said. "Hundreds of things are happening all the time on Pancake Court. Your job is to go out there and get the story!" He waved his hands. "Go! Discover! Write!"

"It's almost night," said Bean, stalling.

"Nice try. It's afternoon. Get out there!" he said. He sounded very enthusiastic. "Find out what makes Pancake Court tick!"

"And then we get our cheese?" Ivy asked.

"Give us news, give us truth, and you will get cheese!" he said, thumping his fist on the kitchen table.

Bean rolled her eyes. "Come on," she said to Ivy. "Let's go get the stupid story."

RATS! SALAMI! WOW!

"I thought this was supposed to keep us off the streets," Bean yelled at the door.

Her father didn't answer. He didn't open the door, either.

"Sheesh." Bean and Ivy walked down the front path to the sidewalk. They looked in one direction. Trees and houses. They looked in the other direction. Trees and houses and a cat.

Ivy sighed and sat down on the sidewalk. "This could take days."

"Months," said Bean. "Years."

The cat walked to the middle of Pancake Court and sat down.

"Cat in Danger?" suggested Ivy. "Is that a story?" She took out her notebook.

The cat licked its leg.

"Clean Cat in Danger," said Bean. She took out her notebook, too.

The cat stood up, gave them an annoyed look, and crossed the street.

"Cat Saved?" said Ivy.

Bean shook her head. "Boring. This is going to be the worst newspaper in the world."

"What if they ask for their money back?" Ivy said gloomily.

"I guess we could give them cheese," said Bean, even more gloomily.

"But it's ours!" said Ivy.

"Not until we write the ding-dang newspaper," said Bean.

They sat some more. Mr. Columbi came out of his house, waved at Ivy and Bean, took a leaf off his car, and went back inside his house.

"Cleanest Car on the Court?" asked Ivy.

"That's not news," said Bean. "His car is always the cleanest."

"Have you ever been in his house?" Ivy asked.

Bean shook her head.

"I wonder if it's as clean as his car," Ivy said.

"Bet it's not," said Bean. She imagined Mr. Columbi's house. "I bet it's really dirty and disgusting. With moldy sandwiches lying on the floor."

"And rats in the sofa," added Ivy.

"Eeeww!" Bean giggled. "He probably eats food out of his shoes because all his plates are dirty."

"There's never a speck of dirt on his car," said Ivy, "because he wants everyone to *think* he's clean."

"His dirty house is his secret," Bean said.

"Mr. Columbi's Dirty Secret," said Ivy.

Bean looked at Ivy. "Now *that's* news."

Ivy smiled. "We'll have to sneak."

"Easy-peasy," said Bean. "If we get caught, we'll say my dad made us do it."

+ + + + + +

Looking into Mr. Columbi's house really was easy-peasy. It was Ivy who found the wheelbarrow in the backyard, and it was Bean who found the wooden box next to the garage. Put the box in the wheelbarrow, and ta-da! A perfect view into Mr. Columbi's living room. Oh look, there was his kitchen, too.

"No rats in the sofa," whispered Ivy, holding tight to the windowsill.

"Maybe they're inside the pillows," hissed Bean below.

"Well, he's sleeping on the sofa," Ivy hissed back. "He wouldn't do that if there were rats, would he?"

"You never know," said Bean. "What about moldy sandwiches?"

"There's a sandwich," said Ivy. "It could be moldy."

"Is it on the floor or in a shoe?"

"It's on a plate," Ivy said. "But there are crumbs everywhere. And, yuck, there's a lot of salami on the floor."

"Salami?"

"That's what it looks like."

"What about the kitchen?" asked Bean.

"I see some plates in the sink," Ivy reported. "And a jar without a lid. He left his oven door open. That's kind of dirty, I think."

"It's dirty enough for me," said Bean. "And he's probably sleeping on the sofa because his bed is full of rats." She wrote "Mr. Columbi's Dirty Secret" in her notebook.

Ivy climbed down from the box and the wheelbarrow. Her eyes were shining. "So that's how you get the story," she said. "This is going to be fun!"

GUESS THE NAKED BABY

They figured that Mr. Columbi wouldn't mind if they borrowed his box. After all, he was fast asleep. Why would he need a box? They carried it over to Dino and Crummy Matt's house and set it against the wall where they thought the kitchen was. They wanted to see how much food Crummy Matt ate.

"Think how big he is," Ivy said. "I bet he eats twenty pounds of food a day."

"I bet their shelves are breaking," said Bean.

"I bet they have two refrigerators."

"Two refrigerators is news for sure," said Bean, climbing onto the box. Luckily, the kitchen window wasn't very far off the ground. Unluckily, the box fell over when she stood on it.

"Ow, *ow*, OW!" Bean yelled, rolling around in the dirt.

"Shh!" whispered Ivy. "They'll hear us!" She sat on top of Bean and covered her mouth with her hand.

"MMMMMMM!" Bean yelled inside Ivy's hand.

Suddenly Dino's head poked out the kitchen window. "Whatcha doing?" he asked.

"Bean fell off the box," Ivy explained.

"Look at my elbow!" yelled Bean. There was blood. Not much. But some.

Dino looked at the box. "Were you looking in our window?" he asked.

"Yes!" said Bean. She kicked the box.

Ivy nudged her warningly, but it was too late.

"Why were you looking in our window?" asked Dino.

Bean and Ivy glanced at each other. Should they lie? No, and Bean couldn't think of one anyway. She sighed. "We're making a newspaper."

"We thought your kitchen would make a great story," said Ivy.

Dino looked at her slitty-eyed. "Why?"

Ivy cleared her throat. How could she say this politely? "Because of Matt."

"What about him?" said Dino suspiciously.

"Um. You know. How big he is." Ivy made a circle with her arms.

"What?" Dino looked
confused.

"We were going to
write a story about how
much food he eats,"
said Bean. "We thought
it might be interesting.
That's why we wanted
to look in your kitchen."

"It's not interesting," said Dino. "Matt's big because he's a mutant."

"Bummer," Ivy said.

"We thought he must eat a lot," said Bean.

"Well, he doesn't. He's boring. He's a boring mutant doofus."

Ivy and Bean looked at each other and shook their heads. "No story." They stood. "I guess we should try Sophie's house," said Bean. She was discouraged.

"Wait!" called Dino. They looked up at him. He was smiling. "I've got a great story for you."

"What?"

"It's a picture, really. Does your newspaper have pictures?"

Bean shrugged. "Sure. Pictures are good." Anything that filled up paper was good.

Dino laughed. "I'll go upstairs and get it. It's on my mom's dresser."

+ + + + + +

"We can call it Guess the Naked Baby," said Bean, looking at the picture.

Ivy started laughing. Again. "But everyone will already know it's Crummy Matt. It looks just like him."

"Except he's *naked!*" Bean yelped. A laugh came out her nose. Again.

They were both laughing so hard they had to sit down on the curb to recover. They had already had to sit down on the curb three times. One time, Bean had laughed so hard she fell into the gutter.

"This newspaper is getting good," gasped Ivy.

A HOT STORY

"Boy, I thought I knew everything that happened on Pancake Court," said Bean as they walked away from Sophie W.'s house.

"You know how Ms. Aruba-Tate is always saying how important it is to understand other people?" Ivy said. "I think I understand people a lot more after I look in their windows."

Sophie W.'s mom had had blue goo all over her face. Also, most of her hair was inside a bag, except for some strings poking out the top. She was painting the strings with a paintbrush. It was very interesting.

Bean leaned the box up against Trevor and Ruby's house. Ivy held it there so she wouldn't fall again. Bean stood on top of the box and peered in the window. "It's just their living room," she said, looking at the empty chairs and sofa. "Pretty boring."

"Let's go around back," suggested Ivy.

Ruby and Trevor were twins. They were eight. They didn't go to school. Their mother taught them at home, which meant they did whatever they wanted and then they had to write about it. Ivy and Bean thought the whole thing was completely unfair.

"Bean!" yelled Ruby and Trevor together when they saw Bean's face peeking over their back fence. "Whatcha doing? Come on over!" they yelled.

"We can't," said Bean. "We're working."

"Who's we?"

"Ivy's down here, holding the box," said Bean.

"Hi!" called Ivy.

"Hi, Ivy!" yelled Ruby.

"We'll help you work," said Trevor. "We're going to croak if something doesn't happen soon."

"You can't help. We're making a newspaper and we have to do it ourselves," said Bean.

"Why'd you come over, then?" asked Ruby.

"We were hoping to find something exciting to put in the newspaper," said Bean.

"There's no news here," said Ruby glumly. "Nothing exciting ever happens around here."

"Okay," said Bean. She started to lower herself off the box.

"No! Wait!" yelled Trevor. "Don't go!" He looked around his backyard. "I'll make something exciting happen. Something you can put in your newspaper."

Ruby rolled her eyes. "Dream on."

"No! Watch!" Trevor jumped up and yanked a leaf off a bush. "I can set this leaf on fire without a match." He pulled a magnifying glass out of his pocket and held it over the leaf. "It's magic!" he said.

"No, it's not. It's a magnifying glass," Bean said.

"Still, I'm starting a fire. That's news,"
Trevor insisted. The sun's rays collected on
the glass and shone down on the leaf.

Bean looked down at Ivy. Ivy shrugged. "It's
just a leaf."

The leaf began to smoke.

"I don't think that counts as news," Bean told Trevor.

Trevor looked up at Bean. "What if I light the whole bush on fire?" he asked.

"Then there'll be a hot time in the old town tonight," Bean said. That was a line from a famous song about a fire, but she couldn't remember what came next.

"Fire! Fire! Fire!" yelled Ruby.

Oh yeah, thought Bean. That's the next line.

Except that's not what Ruby meant. Trevor had dropped the smoking leaf on the lawn and now a little bit of grass was smoking, too. Yikes!

"Fire!" yelled Bean.

"Really?" asked Ivy. "Let me see!" She stopped holding the box and jumped up on it.

"Fire!" shouted Ruby.

"Told you I'd make something happen!" yelled Trevor. "Ha!"

"Put it out!" cried Ruby. She ran to get the hose.

"No! It's my fire!" Trevor shouted. "Leave it alone!"

Ruby twisted the faucet and whirled around, drenching the grass, the fence, and Trevor with water.

"HEY! YOU RUINED MY FIRE!" screeched Trevor. "It was news!" He grabbed the hose from Ruby's hand and sprayed her right in the face.

"AAAAAAaaaaaah!" shrieked Ruby.

"Firefighters on Pancake Court?" suggested Ivy, watching Ruby hit Trevor over the head with the hose.

"That's pretty good," said Bean. "Now we have Mr. Columbi's dirt, Sophie's mom, Trevor and Ruby, and"—she giggled—"Crummy Matt!"

Trevor was stuffing wet grass down Ruby's T-shirt. She was kicking his shin.

"That's only four," said Ivy. "I think we should get one more. Five seems more like a real newspaper."

"Okay," said Bean. "Let's go see what Jake the Teenager is doing."

Trevor and Ruby's mother charged down the back stairs, shouting, "STOP THAT RIGHT NOW!!"

Ivy and Bean quietly climbed down from their box and walked down the driveway as

the shouting continued
behind them.

"I wish I were
homeschooled," Ivy
said. "Don't you?"

FACING THE MUSIC

It was hard to tell which of the teenagers in the garage was Jake the Teenager. They were all big, they were all wearing sunglasses, and they were all yelling and kicking each other. They were a band. The name of their band was Ball Control.

Pretty stupid name, Ivy and Bean thought.

"I think Jake's the one in the red shirt," said Bean. The one in the red shirt was telling everyone else to be quiet, only he didn't say be quiet. He said something else. A lot.

Finally, the other teenagers stopped kicking each other and yelling. Jake the Teenager stood in front of a microphone. "Ah-one, ah-two, ah-three, ah-four!" he said, and then he began to scream.

All the other teenagers began to scream, too. They pounded on their instruments and screamed and screamed.

It was the loudest thing in the world.

Ivy and Bean plugged their ears. They scrunched their eyes. They hunched their shoulders. No matter what they did, it was still the loudest thing in the world.

Then it stopped.

Slowly, Bean unplugged her ears. She unscrunched her eyes. Then she unhunched her shoulders.

Oops. Jake the Teenager was standing on the other side of the window, looking at them.

"Hi," said Bean.

"Hi," he said. After a second, he asked, "What are you doing?"

Bean thought fast. "Listening to your cool band!" she said enthusiastically.

Jake the Teenager took his sunglasses off. "Not bad, huh?" he said.

"Totally!" said Bean.

He nodded. He seemed to be waiting for more.

"Totally awesome!" said Bean.

"But you were plugging your ears," he said.

"It was loud, but it was great," Bean explained.

"What was the name of that great song?" asked Ivy.

"They liked it!" Jake the Teenager yelled over his shoulder. "That one was 'Lizard Hurricane.'"

"Oh boy, we sure liked that song," Bean said. She shook her head as if she were amazed at how much she liked the song.

"Wanna hear the rest?" asked Jake. "We got six songs."

"We would for sure, except we're working," said Bean. "We're writing a newspaper about Pancake Court."

"Dude!" said Jake the Teenager. "Write about our band! Write, like, a music review, you know, about how awesome we are!"

"Sure," said Ivy. "No problem."

"Sure," repeated Bean.

"The next one's called 'Nebulizer,'" he said. "You're gonna love it."

"We have to get writing," said Ivy.

"Deadlines," said Bean, trying to look like she wished she could hear his song. "Got to go!"

"Say we'll play for parties," he yelled after them as they went down the driveway.

"Dude! Trust me!" said Bean, waving.

"Wow, you can really talk teenager," said Ivy.

"Anyone can do it," said Bean modestly. "You just have to practice."

It was getting late. "We'd better go to your house and get started," Ivy said to Bean. She thought for a moment. "You don't think your dad ate the cheese, do you?"

Bean shook her head. "He wouldn't do that." She looked worried. "At least, I don't think so."

"Grown-ups like cheese," Ivy said.

"We'd better work fast."

THE PANCAKE FLIPS

They wrote *The Flipping Pancake* until it was time for Ivy to go home for dinner. The next day after school, they rushed home to finish it.

By the time they were done, Bean's kitchen table was covered with paper, pencils, scissors, erasers, glue sticks, and mess-ups. In the middle of the table was one perfect copy of *The Flipping Pancake*.

Ivy and Bean looked at it admiringly. It was beautiful. At the top, Bean had drawn a pancake with little lines coming out of it to show that it was jumping in the air. Around the pancake, she had written in her best printing *The Fliping Pancake*. So what if she had forgotten the other *P*? It still looked great.

Below the title was the first story, the one about the rats and salami in Mr. Columbi's house. Ivy had decided it was mean to say he was dirty, so she had called it "Mr. Columbi's Secret."

After that came Guess the Naked Baby. They had pasted the picture of Crummy Matt to the paper. There he was, drooling and smiling on a white rug, his rear end waving in the air. Ivy and Bean had almost stopped laughing about it by now. But not quite.

Bean had drawn a picture of Sophie's mom with her hair in a bag and blue goo on her face. Beneath it, she had written, "Mrs. W. is up to something!" That was really all she could say, since she didn't know what Sophie's mom was doing.

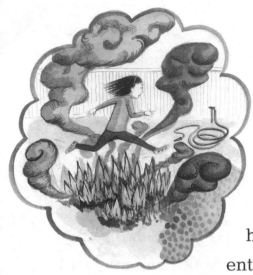

Together Ivy and Bean had written the exciting story about the fire at Trevor and Ruby's. In fact, they made it a little more exciting than it really had been. They said the entire backyard burst into flames. They also said that Ruby had saved Trevor's life by running over flames to get the hose. "People like to read exciting stories," Bean said.

Down at the very bottom of the page, Ivy had written about Ball Control. She said that they were famous for "Lizard Hurricane," and if you wanted to drown out a loud noise, you could ask them over to your house for a party.

The story looked a little skimpy, so she also wrote that there were no bad words in their songs. She said that a lot of the other music that Jake the Teenager listened to had bad words in it. She put down the first letter of the really amazingly bad word they had heard. Then she drew an arrow and wrote, "Not in Ball Control songs!"

There had been just enough room to squeeze in a weather report down at the bottom. Bean had drawn a picture of the sun.

"Wow," said Ivy. "I can't believe we made such a great paper. It looks so *real.*"

"We could get famous for this," said Bean. "I mean"—she picked up the paper—"not many kids could do a whole newspaper all by themselves."

Ivy nodded. "Let's copy it on my mom's copier," she said. "Do you think we should give a copy to Sophie W.'s mom, even if she didn't pay for it? You know, because she's in it?"

"No way!" said Bean.

"But she might give us money when she sees how great it is," Ivy explained.

"Oh. Right," said Bean. "Yeah. Also we have to make one for my dad, so he'll give us our cheese back."

"He's going to be surprised," said Ivy.

Bean nodded. "They're all going to be surprised."

+ + + + + +

And they were surprised, but not exactly in the way that Ivy and Bean had imagined.

After they delivered *The Flipping Pancake* to Jean, Jake the Teenager's dad, Ruby and

Trevor's mom, Liana and Katy's father, Dino and Crummy Matt's mom, Mrs. W., and Mr. Columbi, they brought a copy to Bean's dad. He was on the living room couch, reading a magazine.

"Here," said Bean. "Can we have our cheese now?"

"You just hang on to your engines, kiddo," he said. He put down his magazine and picked up *The Flipping Pancake.* "If I see that you two put real work into it, you can have your cheese. There are standards that you have to—" He stopped talking and made a funny sound.

"Which one are you reading?" asked Ivy.

"Mr. Columbi's Secret," he said, but his voice was funny. He was snorting. Or choking.

Or something. "Is that *Matt*?" he asked in a strangled voice. "Does he *know*?"

Bean looked at Ivy and shrugged. "Probably, by now."

Her father wasn't paying attention. "What is this picture of Sheila?" That was Mrs. W.'s name. "What's she doing?"

"Got me," said Bean. "She was painting her hair. I don't know what she had on her face."

He read on. "The twins set their yard on fire? When? Does their mom know?"

"Oh sure. She was there," said Bean.

Bean's dad stopped reading and frowned. "How did you get all this, anyway?"

Bean put her hands on her hips. "Look. We did exactly what you told us to do. We went out and found the story."

He opened his mouth but he didn't say anything. For a second, he just stared at her. And then he started laughing. He laughed really, really hard. He almost fell off the couch.

"You do that, too," said Ivy.

"I know. I inherited it," said Bean. They watched Bean's dad laugh for a while, and then Bean said again, "Can we have our cheese now?"

"What?" Dad said, wiping his eyes.

She said it again, loudly.

"Lowfat Belldeloon cheese in a special just-for-you serving size," said Ivy, in case he had forgotten.

He was still laughing a little, but he got up. "It's all yours, girls. You have earned your cheese." He walked toward the kitchen.

"We won!" whispered Ivy and Bean together as they followed.

"Now, kids," said Bean's dad, handing them their little red bags of cheese. "Even though I think *The Flipping—Flipping—*" he started laughing again and covered his eyes. "*The Flipping Pancake* is a masterpiece, but it just might be too, um, powerful for some people. Maybe Sheila wouldn't like people to know that she paints her hair. For example."

"But she does," said Bean, carefully selecting the best ball of cheese.

"But maybe she wouldn't want *other* people to know that," he said. "So maybe we should just keep *The Flipping Pancake* here inside our own house."

Ivy and Bean looked at each other. Grown-ups were so weird. "We already made copies and delivered them," Bean said. "You said we took their money and we had to deliver what we promised. So we did."

The doorbell rang.

THE WHOLE BALL OF WAX

An hour later, Ivy and Bean were lying on Bean's trampoline, squishing their beautiful red wax. Squish, squish, squish.

They had come outside when the kitchen got too crowded with grown-ups. Ruby and Trevor's mom had made them promise never to show *The Flipping Pancake* to Ruby and Trevor's dad. Mrs. W. had stopped by with a dollar for her copy, just like Ivy had expected.

But she had also asked them to stop looking in her window. Mr. Columbi did, too. And Crummy Matt's mom had actually wanted his photo back again. She had even paid for it.

"Two dollars, just to get a picture back." Ivy shook her head. "Doesn't seem worth it to me."

"She's his *mom*," said Bean. "She probably thinks it's cute. I think she's mad at Dino, though."

"Ruby and Trevor are grounded, their mom said." Ivy frowned. "But if you're at home all the time anyway, how can you tell?"

"I don't know," said Bean.

For a while, they lay peacefully on the trampoline, squishing their wax.

Then Bean sat up. Something was shuffling on the other side of her fence. "Do you hear that?" Bean whispered.

"What?" whispered Ivy. Then she heard it. "Is it a bear?" She hoped it was.

It wasn't a bear. It was whispering. Ivy and Bean slid quietly off the trampoline and tiptoed toward the fence. There was a lot of shuffling going on out there. And a grunt. The grunt sounded familiar. It was Crummy Matt's grunt.

"I'll get 'em," he was saying. He was talking as softly as he could, but that wasn't very soft.

Ivy bugged her eyes at Bean. Get 'em? What did that mean? It sounded bad.

"No," whispered a voice that sounded like Dino. "You grab them and I'll get 'em. But we got to go quick, because Mom's going to find out we're gone pretty soon."

There was that stuff about getting them again. *Yikes*, Bean mouthed to Ivy.

"I brought blue paint," whispered another voice. "If you hold them, I'll paint them." That sounded like Sophie W. Like a mad Sophie W.

Blue paint? Ivy put her hands over her cheeks. A blue face would be okay, but not a blue face painted by a mad person.

"Okay. You have a camera?" It sounded like Trevor.

"Trevor, give me that magnifying glass. You can't light them on fire." Ruby's voice was very high and squeaky.

Bean grabbed Ivy's arm and yanked. Time for a getaway. But where? For a second, they just zipped wildly around the yard.

"Who says I can't?" Trevor snarled. "We're grounded already!"

"Trevor, give it here!"

"Shhh! They'll hear!" said Sophie W.

Ivy looked at Bean. *Inside,* she mouthed.

No. Wait, mouthed Bean. She held up her wax. Quickly, she squished it flat and stuck it under her nose. Then she lay down next to the trampoline. *Come on*, she beckoned to Ivy. Then she closed her eyes.

"Come on!" grunted Matt. The gate latch rattled. They were coming in.

Ivy smashed her wax flat against her forehead and dropped to the ground next to Bean with her eyes closed.

The gate opened and banged shut.

"Whoa!" said Trevor.

"Oh my gosh!" whispered Sophie W.

"What happened to them?" Dino said. "Is that *blood*?"

"Uh," grunted Crummy Matt. "I gotta go."

There was the sound of the gate opening and closing again.

"They must have fallen off that trampoline," Ruby whispered.

"Maybe they're only fainted," said Sophie.

"We could check," said Ruby.

They didn't.

"Should we tell the grown-ups?" Dino asked quietly.

There was a long silence.

Then Sophie W. sighed. "Okay. I'll do it."

"Let's go," said Dino.

The gate banged again.

Footsteps went away, down the driveway.

Bean opened one eye. "They're gone," she whispered. She peeled the wax from her lip and nudged Ivy. "Pretty good, huh?"

Ivy giggled. "They thought we were dead!" She took the wax off her forehead. "I love this stuff!"

From far away inside the house, they heard the doorbell ring, but they didn't answer it. They knew who it was, and besides, they were busy jumping.

A second later, they heard the sound of Bean's dad running. They watched as he flew out the back door and skidded across the porch. "Are you okay?" he yelled.

Ivy and Bean stopped jumping. "We're fine," said Bean.

"Sophie said you were hurt," he panted.

"Oh, that Sophie," said Ivy. "She was probably just joking."

"No," he began. And then he stopped and frowned. "Do you think this has something to do with *The Flipping Pancake?*"

Bean and Ivy looked at each other and then back at Bean's dad. They made their eyes big. "How could it?" Ivy asked.

"Dad," said Bean. "Thanks for giving us the idea to do a newspaper. It was really fun."

He coughed. "Any time. I'm full of good ideas."

Bean reached into her pocket and pulled out a circle of cheese. It was a little bit fuzzy. "Here." She held it out to her dad. "This is your thank-you present."

"You can have mine, too," said Ivy.

"What?" said Bean's dad. "I thought you loved this cheese."

"Nah," said Bean.

"Actually," said Ivy, "the cheese is kind of gross."

"But you might like it," said Bean.

Bean's dad turned around and walked into the house without saying a word.

"What's the matter with him?" whispered Ivy.

Bean shrugged. "Maybe he's tired." She set the circle of cheese on the edge of the trampoline and held up her wax. So did Ivy.

Squish, squish, squish.

The End